Whisker Winks:
The Magical Life of Deano Martini

TESSA CERVANTES

First published by Cat Pack Publishing 2025 Copyright © 2025 by Tessa Cervantes

First edition

Paperback ISBN : 978-1-968404-44-4

Cover art by Tessa Cervantes

This book was professionally typeset on Reedsy.

Find out more at reedsy.com

To Samy, Frankie, and Deano, also known as "The Cat Pack," thank you for inspiring me to write and tell your stories. We are so blessed to have you in our lives.

To Deano Martini, our FIP survivor, thank you for teaching us not to ever give up.

To Darin, thank you for being my partner in this magical ride. You are my constant source of love and support.

To Michelle and Gabby, I love you to the moon and back.

And to all the shelter pets, may you find your forever-loving home.

Table of Contents

Acknowledgments

From morning sunbaths to evening purrs, each and every stretch and nap has taught me to cherish life's simple pleasures. Their whiskers twitch through joy and challenges, providing a tranquility that resonates within me. Whether it is Samy David Jr.'s playful antics, Frankie Sinatro's soulful gazes, or Deano Martini's gentle purring, each moment highlights the profound impact our pets have on our hearts.

Writing *Whisker Winks: The Magical Life of Deano Martini* has been a journey of love, healing, and magic. I could not have done it alone.

To the Cat Pack—Samy, Frankie, and Deano—I express my gratitude for your daily inspiration through your unique personalities and bravery. Your presence has imparted valuable lessons in the importance of rest and adaptability.

To Deano, our FIP survivor, thank you for showing perseverance. Despite the many challenges faced, each morning is greeted with gratitude and happiness.

To Darin, thanks for your support, love, and patience. You are the best Cat Daddy.

To Dina, Joe, and Erin, our sincere gratitude for agreeing to care for our cats during our vacation.

To Marisol, Tony, and Barbara, we extend our thanks for your frequent visits. Samy, Frankie, and Deano greatly appreciate your presence in our home.

To Ruthie, I express my profound appreciation for your unwavering support and encouragement. Your kindness and simplicity have been a remarkable source of inspiration.

To Tammy, our wonderful neighbor, thank you. You are a blessing to us and to Billie.

To everyone who has ever opened their heart to a shelter pet, your kindness inspires this world. And finally, to every reader holding this book in their hands—thank you. I hope this story brings you comfort, smiles, and a little sparkle of feline magic. Lastly to all shelter pets, may you find loving and permanent homes.

Chapter 1: The Cat Pack

It all started on a quiet afternoon visit to our favorite local bookstore.

As we approached, we noticed it was one of those special days with extra events to attract more visitors. The entrance was decorated with photos of various cats.

I glanced at Darin and smiled, thinking this was a double treat. Inside, friendly volunteers greeted us warmly. A table was beautifully arranged with colorful flyers and a large sign reading "Local No-Kill Cat Shelter: Adoptions Today!" Being a cat lover, I couldn't resist chatting with the volunteers and checking out the cats available for adoption. Tiny kittens filled the cages, wiggling and meowing for attention.

One cage caught my eye immediately.

ADOPT
ADOPTION

Inside were two kittens: a charming tuxedo cat and a timid orange tabby. The tuxedo sat calm and composed, gently wrapping his paws around his nervous brother, who looked frightened and uncertain in the bustling noise of the bookstore.

While Darin wandered off to explore the shop, I stayed behind, chatting with the volunteers. Curious about the tuxedo cat, I asked for more details, and they shared sweet stories about how gentle he was and how he always looked out for his brother. Smiling, I turned to the girl at the booth to inquire about the adoption process. I quickly texted Darin to come over and meet this handsome tuxedo cat.

A few minutes later, Darin walked back toward me, and I led him to the kennel. He took one look at the tuxedo cat and immediately said yes.

I bent down toward the cage, ready to celebrate, but my heart caught in my throat. The tuxedo cat clung tightly to his brother, his eyes silently pleading with me:

If you choose me, you have to choose him too.

I gave Darin the most dramatic puppy-dog eyes I could manage. He chuckled softly and said, "Yes."

And just like that, we adopted both brothers.

As we carried the kennel to the car, I could swear I saw a glimmer of happiness in the tuxedo cat's eyes, as if he knew his little family was staying together.

On the drive home though, a new concern crept in—Samy, our sixteen-year-old senior cat and the undisputed king of the house. How would he feel about two rambunctious kittens disrupting his peaceful realm?

When we arrived, we kept the brothers safely inside their kennel while Darin and I sat with Samy. We hugged him, reassured him, and promised that no matter what, he would always be the leader of our little family.

Samy listened quietly, sitting by the window like a wise old owl. Finally, we opened the kennel door. The kittens wobbled out, wide-eyed and curious. Samy watched… and he did not look impressed.

As we watched the two little brothers explore their new home, we realized they needed names that would fit into our family. Our wise and slightly grumpy elder cat was named Samy David Jr., a name as legendary as his spirit. It felt only right to carry on the tradition.

We decided to name the handsome tuxedo Frankie Sinatro—cool, charming, and protective, just like a real crooner.

And the sweet orange tabby with the soft eyes? He became Deano Martini—a little laid-back, a little shy, but full of heart.

And just like that, "The Cat Pack" was born—Frankie Sinatro, Deano Martini, and Samy David Jr., also known as Sam Wise, leading his new brothers into a world brimming with wonder. Together they walked, tails high and hearts open.

Chapter 2: Samy Smoky Meow

The house felt quieter than usual. Samy, our wise old orange tabby, had once been the proud ruler of every windowsill, every sunbeam, and every pillow. For sixteen years, he was our baby—pampered, adored, and never having to share a single toy or treat.

But now, things had changed.

Two curious little kittens, Deano and Frankie, arrived as bundles of joy and energy, tumbling through the house like tiny tornadoes. Samy watched from afar, his green eyes thoughtful, unsure. It wasn't long before he withdrew into a quiet corner, barely eating, sleeping more than usual. His once-bold meow turned faint, and his spirit dimmed.

We knew something was wrong. We bundled him gently into his carrier and took him to our trusted vet, Dr. J. She examined him carefully and diagnosed Samy with an upper respiratory infection—an illness likely made worse by the emotional stress of sudden change. She sent us home with medication and soft reassurances.

CAT
CARE

As Samy rested, something magical unfolded. The kittens—so young, so full of life—seemed to understand. They didn't jump on him or beg for his attention. Instead, they stayed nearby, quietly waiting. Frankie often curled near the edge of Samy's favorite spot, just close enough to be seen but not touched. Deano gently placed his hair-claw clip toy nearby, like an offering of friendship.

Slowly, Samy began to recover. He nibbled his food again. He ventured back to the perch by the window. And one sunny morning, we heard a sound that made us smile—it was Samy, letting out a low, raspy meow that sounded like a little old man with a tiny cigar. It was so unexpected, so Samy, we couldn't help but laugh.

His voice had changed, but his heart had opened. In the days that followed, the Cat Pack began to play. A game of chasing here, a shared sunbeam there. Samy wasn't just healing, he was rediscovering joy. The kittens had reminded him how it felt to be young, and Samy had begun to accept them—not just as new housemates... but as family.

Chapter 3: The Diagnosis

It started with small changes. Deano, usually full of sparkle and spunk, began sleeping more than usual. He stopped chasing sunbeams and pawing at dangling strings. Most concerning of all, he ignored his favorite toy, Mama's hair claw clip. The glint in his amber eyes dulled, and his once-playful pounces became slow shuffles. Something wasn't right.

Our hearts filled with worry. He was still just a kitten. How could this be happening?

Darin, always calm in a crisis, immediately called Dr. J's office. We scheduled appointments for all three cats: Samy for a follow-up checkup, Frankie for his very first vet visit, and Deano to figure out what was stealing his spark.

Samy's visit went smoothly. His recovery from the URI was going well, and despite his new smoky-voiced meow, Dr. J assured us that Samy David Jr. was in good health. Frankie's exam, however, revealed a surprise: a heart murmur.

Dr. J carefully listened to Frankie Sinatro's tiny chest, then drew blood for lab work and scheduled an ultrasound to learn more. His test results came back, and Dr. J reassured us that there was nothing to worry about at this time.

Then came Deano.

The room grew still as Dr. J examined him thoroughly. She looked concerned as she listened to Deano Martini's heartbeat, felt his body, and observed his lethargy.

After some time, she gently delivered the heartbreaking news: Deano showed signs of FIP, Feline Infectious Peritonitis—a rare and often deadly disease.

Dr. J explained that she didn't treat FIP herself, but she referred us to a local FIP warrior group that had helped other families. They could guide us through the process. Even with the referral in hand, leaving the clinic that day felt like walking through a storm. We were quiet. Afraid. Devastated.

That evening, we gathered in the living room, standing by the window as the last light of day faded into the sky.

Deano lay quietly on a soft pillow nearby, his little body tired but still full of hope. Frankie sat close to him, keeping watch, while Samy perched by the edge of the couch, his wise green eyes never leaving Deano's side. We talked about everything Dr. J had said—the diagnosis, the treatment, the risks, the hope.

Darin and I stood close together, quietly making a promise without even needing to say it out loud. We were going to fight for him. No matter what it takes.

Back home, Darin wasted no time. He immediately began making calls, searching online, reaching out to the group. Within hours, we had information: there was a treatment plan, but it would take 84 days. The first 30 days would involve daily injections, followed by 54 days of oral medication. The cost was high, and the path ahead uncertain—but we didn't hesitate. We chose to fight for Deano.

He wasn't just a kitten. He was magic. He was love. And no matter what it took, we were going to help him survive.

Chapter 4: The First Spark

The house was heavy with silence the morning we gave Deano his first injection. It was the start of a long, uncertain journey—84 days of hope and healing. We held our breath as the tiny needle delivered its magic, praying it would bring our brave little warrior back to us.

And then, something shifted.

After 48 hours, we noticed a change. A small one, but unmistakable. Deano's eyes had a flicker of alertness again. He sat up, stretched slowly, and looked around. By evening, he was sniffing at his favorite toy. And the next morning, he was back to teasing his brother with light taps of his paw.

We couldn't believe it.

To celebrate, we brought home a new toy: a round relay track with bright balls that spun in circles when pawed. It was an instant hit. Deano was hooked—his paws smacked the ball again and again, sending it racing around the track. Frankie joined in, his tuxedo paws adding flair. Even Samy gave it a gentle nudge before watching the chaos unfold from his perch with a knowing look. The house buzzed with life again. Laughter returned. So did the games. Deano chased the crinkle ball, flipped upside down mid-pounce, and even tried to sit on the toy track just to block the others from playing. His energy was back, and so was our joy.

Frankie, ever the protector, now watched Deano with relief. Samy, the quiet observer—the leader of the pack—returned to his window perch, but his eyes held warmth again.

Deano was back.

The first spark of hope had turned into a full-blown flame.

Chapter 5: Where's the Clip?

On a bright and cheerful morning, Deano Martini awoke with a sense of adventure bubbling inside him. The sun streamed through the window, casting playful shadows that danced across the floor. Today was a perfect day for his favorite game, "Where's the clip?" With a quick stretch and a flick of his tail, Deano bounded to the living room, eager to start the fun. He would toss the clip and run after it, and he would toss it again and again. One time, he tossed it so high he couldn't find it. He searched everywhere.

Deano finally spotted the clip wedged beneath the couch. With a triumphant leap, he pounced, his little body soaring through the air. "I found it!" he exclaimed, proudly clutching the clip in his mouth. He tossed it again and again, and this time, the clip rolled under the cabinet.

Deano started pacing back and forth. His meow sounded different—a sound of frustration. Seeing her little boy's distress, Tessa called out to Darin. "Can you help him? His clip is somewhere under the cabinet."

Darin got down on the floor and, with a smile, reached under the cabinet. A moment later, he triumphantly held up the small brown clip. Deano perked up instantly, tail flicking. He leapt to his feet, eyes locked on the clip in Darin's hand.

Darin was on his knees, holding the elusive hair claw clip, a small, shiny object that sparkled like treasure. Deano's eyes widened with anticipation as he prepared for the game. Samy, perched on the arm of the couch, watched with a wise smile, while Frankie cheered from a nearby cushion, his tuxedo fur gleaming in the light.

"Okay, Deano! Ready? Where's the clip?" Darin said with a wink, tossing the clip into the air. Deano sprang into action, his paws dancing across the floor as he followed the glint of the clip. He darted left, then right, his heart racing with excitement.

"Look out, Deano!" Frankie shouted, bouncing up and down on his cushion. "It's right behind you!"

"Remember, my young friend," Samy called out, his voice calm and smooth, "patience and focus are the keys. Trust your instincts." Deano nodded, taking a moment to gather himself and concentrate on the game. With renewed determination, he resumed the hunt.

"Good boy, Deano!" Darin clapped his hands, and Frankie jumped down to give his brother a playful nuzzle. Even Samy couldn't help but chuckle, his deep voice resonating with warmth. "Well done, little warrior. You've proven your skills today."

As the game continued, laughter echoed throughout the house. Deano felt a warm glow in his heart, surrounded by love and support from his family. No matter how many times they played, each game brought them closer, reminding him of the joy found in friendship and play. This moment brought such joy to our hearts. Our little warrior, what an angel.

"Fetch, Deano!" Darin said, tossing the clip again.

Chapter 6: The Great Leash Adventure

It all started with a couple of tiny harnesses and a lot of hope. We decided it was time to teach Frankie and Deano how to walk on a leash. The idea of exploring the world beyond the windows was exciting, but the training? Not so much. We hoped they would like it, just like Samy.

Deano flopped dramatically the first time the harness went on, pretending his legs had turned to noodles. Frankie slunk low to the ground, clearly offended by the strange contraption now hugging his tuxedo fur. There were a lot of wiggles, tumbles, and confused looks. But we didn't give up.

With gentle encouragement (and a few treats), they began to get used to the feel of the harness. We practiced in the living room first, then ventured into the backyard. Every step was a victory.

Samy, ever the calm elder, strolled beside them like a wise tour guide. "You'll love it," he seemed to say with a flick of his tail. "There's a whole world out there—sunlight, breezes, birds!"

Soon, the day came for their very first real walk. We clipped their leashes on, stepped outside the front door, and… magic.

Deano sniffed the air, his tail high with curiosity. Frankie batted at a leaf tumbling across the sidewalk, and Samy led the way with a regal strut, *the three of them forming a purring parade—whiskers, paws, and wonder.* The Cat Pack stepped into the world, ready for their next grand adventure.

The world was full of fascinating sights and smells. There were chirping birds in bushes, mysterious rustling from behind fences, and even a butterfly that made all three cats freeze in awe.

By the time we returned home, they were tired but thrilled. Their first leash walk was a success, and the beginning of many adventures to come. They had conquered the harness, and now, the world was theirs to explore.

Chapter 7: The Visitor in the Shadows

The back porch was no longer just a porch. With a few weekends of building, measuring, and a lot of teamwork, we turned it into a dream come true for our cats: the "Catio." What happens in the Catio stays in the Catio (nah).

Windows lined every side, letting in golden rays of sun. We added cat perches, cozy beds, and an assortment of dangling toys. There were climbing posts and cozy corners, and the space felt alive with possibilities. Deano darted from perch to perch, Frankie stretched out lazily on a sun-warmed ledge, and Samy watched the world with quiet majesty from his favorite corner.

The Catio became their happy place—a safe slice of the outdoors filled with fluttering birds, rustling leaves, and the occasional dog trotting down the back alley. Every morning and evening, it was their favorite routine.

But one day, something changed.

From the far side of the yard, a mysterious figure appeared. He was brown, with wild, scruffy fur and fierce eyes—a stray cat that looked almost like a little bobcat. He moved with silent confidence and watched from the shadows just beyond the edge of the catio.

Samy spotted him first. His body tensed, and a deep, unfamiliar growl rumbled in his throat. His tail puffed up, and he stood firmly in front of Frankie and Deano, placing himself between them and the stranger outside. His usual calm demeanor was gone; this was Samy, the leader of the pack and the protector. His low meows grew louder, more intense.

Darin, hearing the warning sounds, rushed out to the Catio. The moment the door creaked open, the mysterious cat bolted, vanishing into the alley like a shadow slipping away.

Darin crouched beside Samy, gently stroking his back. "It's okay, big guy. You did good. He's gone." Samy finally relaxed, though his eyes stayed locked on the spot where the bobcat-like cat had disappeared.

Darin led everyone back inside the house. Deano and Frankie looked at each other, feeling protected and safe around Samy.

Even in paradise, a little wildness sometimes finds its way in. But with Samy on watch, we knew the kittens were in good hands—I mean, good paws.

Chapter 8: The Garden Guests

It was a warm, golden afternoon, and I was in the garden planting more herbs—mint, basil, rosemary, and a few tiny sprigs of catnip. Just beyond the flower beds, the grass swayed gently as Samy, Frankie, and Deano rolled happily in the sunshine. The air was full of fresh earth, soft breezes, and the excited chirps of little birds hopping around for seeds.

Samy lay calmly, eyes half-closed, tail flicking now and then as he listened. But for Deano and Frankie, this was an entirely new thrill. Their ears twitched. Their bodies tensed. Then—pounce! They dashed toward the birds, sending feathers fluttering and wings flapping. The startled birds flew off, but some returned moments later, determined to get their share of seeds.

> *"Hey! Be nice to the birds!" I called from the herb patch, shaking my trowel. Samy simply blinked at me, then turned back to his sunbathing.*

Then came a sound, a soft rustle in the bushes. All three cats perked up. They approached the bushes slowly, their tails swaying, eyes wide. Peering through the leaves, they found a familiar sight: the mysterious brown cat who looked like a little bobcat. He stood still, cautious but curious. The three cats stood quietly, then slowly stepped forward, noses twitching as they exchanged sniffs.

And then, another shadow emerged.

From deeper in the garden came a much larger stray, a black-and-white cat with a serious look in his eyes and a rough, rugged exterior. He didn't hiss or growl, just sat nearby, observing. Frankie and Deano lay down slowly. Samy stayed alert but calm. For a few moments, they all simply coexisted—five cats under the fading sun.

Eventually, the two strays dashed off into the neighborhood. The sky began to darken. I dusted my hands off and called them in. The front door stayed open, with just the screen closed. The boys settled down, watching the porch closely, tails flicking with anticipation.

They were waiting for Papa. As his car pulled up and his footsteps crunched the gravel path, all three perked up with excitement.

Tonight, they had so much to tell him about birds, bushes, and two mysterious visitors in the garden.

Chapter 9: Billie and Oreo

It started one evening, just as the sky began to blush with sunset. I pulled into the driveway after work, tired but content, when something moved near the rose bushes. There he was—the mysterious brown cat who looked like a bobcat. He paused for a moment, then gracefully slipped into the shadows.

But that was only the beginning.

From then on, the bobcat-like cat began appearing regularly in the front yard. He never came too close, always keeping a respectful distance, but he was there. Watching. Waiting. We named him Billie.

Eventually, I began leaving food out for Billie. Just a small bowl of kibble on the front patio. He'd sneak over, ears twitching, and begin to eat. But he was never alone.

Behind him, a larger cat with bold black-and-white patches would linger in the background, always watching. He never approached the food. He never intervened. But he was always there, keeping an eye on Billie like a silent guardian. We named him Oreo.

Soon, feeding them became a routine. Every morning and evening, I'd leave out food, and the two strays would appear—sometimes together, sometimes Billie is alone. Sometimes, Oreo would sit across the yard, regal and watchful.

The Cat Pack would sit inside by the screen door or front window, tails flicking as they watched the visitors. Sometimes, when I cracked open the front door just enough, the three house cats would take turns sniffing curiously or playfully pawing at Billie through the screen.

I even left a few toys on the patio—a soft mouse, a crinkle ball, a feather wand. Billie would occasionally bat at them with a shy paw, his wild edge softening. Oreo never joined the play, but we noticed his eyes following every movement.

It became a rhythm. A quiet friendship. A shared space. Until one day, Billie didn't come.

Morning turned to evening, and there was no sign of him. A day passed. Then two. Then weeks. We left the food out anyway. Deano, Frankie, and Samy sat by the window each day, waiting. Oreo came by a few times alone, sitting at a distance, like always.

But Billie was gone. We didn't know where he went or if he was okay.

All we could do was hope and wait.

Chapter 10: Billie's Secret

Billie came back—but she wasn't alone.

We heard soft meows before we saw them. Four tiny kittens tumbled into view, following closely behind her. They were beautiful and delicate, each one with different fur patches, like little paintings brought to life. Billie, it turned out, was not a bobcat boy at all. She was a young mama, and she had chosen our front porch as her safe place.

After she ate, Billie curled up in a warm corner of the porch and let her kittens nurse. It was such a tender moment, and we all watched from the window, our hearts full. She had brought extra joy into our lives, and the kittens added a whole new level of wonder.

Oreo, as usual, watched from a distance. He kept his post nearby, his eyes always on Billie and the kittens. Was he the father? We couldn't be sure. But he was always there, alert and protective, never interfering—just guarding.

Day after day, they came. Billie relaxed more and more around us. Deano, Frankie, and Samy would watch through the screen or sit nearby when Billie came close to the door. It was as if she had become part of the family. We added a cat perch to the front porch, and more blankets, toys, and even a little shelter. Billie had found a home, and she knew it.

We knew it was time. Billie needed to be spayed to ensure her safety and health. So, we gently coaxed her into a carrier and took her to the community vet.

COMMUNITY
VET

That night, the porch felt strangely empty.

Oreo was devastated. He circled the house, checking the front and back doors, the catio, and the windows. He meowed loudly, a mournful call as if asking, *"Where is she?"*

Deano, Frankie, and Samy sat by the window, their eyes full of understanding.

The next day, we brought Billie home. We set her up comfortably in the catio so she could rest safely. But Billie had other plans. Later that evening, we found the door ajar—she had slipped out, vanishing into the night.

Even with all our care, Billie still had a little wild in her. But this time, we knew she wouldn't be gone for long. This porch was her home now. And she had family waiting for her.

Chapter 11: A Stroll Through the Neighborhood

It was a warm, sunny afternoon, and the excitement in the air was palpable. Deano and Frankie, the adventurous duo, were ready for one of their favorite activities—a stroll around the neighborhood. Samy, with his wise and steady presence, took his usual place at the bottom, while Billie led the way, her head held high, proud to be their guide.

As they stepped outside, the world opened before them. Billie led the group down the sunny path. Deano and Frankie sat comfortably, enjoying the view, and not a single argument passed between the brothers.

During their stroll, they encountered a chorus of birds singing in the trees. Deano's ears perked up, and he gazed in awe at the colorful, feathered creatures flitting from branch to branch.

"Look at them, Frankie!" Deano whispered excitedly.

"They're so beautiful!"

As they continued their adventure, they came across people walking their dogs. Some were big and fluffy, while others were small and energetic. Billie walked proudly in front, her confidence shining. She seemed to enjoy showing off her new friends.

A young boy saw them and said, "Your cats are amazing and look so happy!" He smiled as he walked toward The Cat Pack. Deano and Frankie were pleased to meet another person, while Samy remained partially hidden, and Billie stood upright, showing pride.

"Hi, I'm Bruce," the boy said with a big grin. *"These are my cats, Chester and Chico!"* he added proudly, as the kittens looked on with adoration and curiosity. Billie gave a soft chirp in greeting, towering slightly over the tiny newcomers.

The boy gently stroked Samy's fur, and Frankie leaned into the boy's hand, enjoying the attention.

"You're all so cool!" the boy exclaimed, his eyes sparkling.

This moment of connection filled the air with warmth and happiness.

As their stroll came to an end, Deano, Frankie, Samy, and Billie returned home, their hearts full of joy and new memories. They had ventured out into the world, met new friends, and seen the beauty of nature.

With each walk, their bond grew stronger, reminding them of the joy found in shared experiences.

Chapter 12: A Cozy Porch Gathering

After a delightful afternoon of exploration, Deano, Frankie, Samy, and Billie returned home, their hearts full of joy and laughter from their stroll. The sun began to set, casting a warm golden glow over the porch. It was the perfect time to unwind and share stories of their adventure.

As they settled down on the porch, Billie fluffed her fur and looked around.

"Today was so much fun! I loved leading the way and showing you all the different birds," she said, her voice filled with pride. Deano nodded excitedly.

"And that boy who petted us! He thought we were amazing!"

Frankie chimed in, *"I felt like a superstar!"*

Deano had tucked his clip safely in the stroller. He beamed with pride as he showed it to Billie.

Just then, Mama Tessa appeared with a tray of snacks.

"Look what I've brought for my adventurous kittens!" she announced, her eyes twinkling. She set down some crunchy treats and a few small bits of fish, and the cats' eyes widened in delight.

As they munched on their treats, each cat took turns sharing their favorite moments from the day. Samy, with his calm demeanor, said thoughtfully,

"It's wonderful how much joy there is in simply exploring together. Every day is an adventure with all of you."

Billie smiled, "And I loved how everyone cheered for us! It felt like we were in a parade."

Deano added, "Next time, we should bring a little flag to wave!"

Frankie laughed, imagining the spectacle, and everyone joined in the laughter.

As the sun dipped lower in the sky, casting a warm glow over their little porch, the cats felt a sense of contentment.

They were not just friends; they were family, sharing moments of joy, adventure, and delicious snacks.

Chapter 13: Realm of Lost Toys

The next day, with the sun shining brightly, Tessa and Darin decided it was time for some spring cleaning. As they moved furniture and tidied up the house, Deano, Frankie, Samy, and Billie watched with curious eyes from their cozy spots.

While cleaning under the fridge, Tessa spotted something shiny glinting in the corner.

"What's this?" she exclaimed, pulling out a collection of colorful clips and crunchy toys that had long been lost to the realm beneath the fridge.

Deano, Frankie, Samy, and Billie perked up at the sight of the newfound treasures. Their eyes widened with excitement as they rushed over to inspect the colorful finds.

"Look at all this stuff!" Deano exclaimed, his tail flicking with delight.

Deano jumped to catch the first one, while Frankie darted in to snatch another. Billie, wanting her share, playfully pawed at a clip that had landed near her.

Among the treasures, they also found crunchy toys that made delightful sounds when bitten or batted around. The moment they discovered these, the living room transformed into a playground. The cats chased and batted the toys, their laughter filling the air.

The cats imagined a secret world from which these treasures had come—a realm of lost toys where all forgotten things went to have adventures.

"Maybe there's a kingdom where all the lost toys gather!"

Frankie mused.

After a fun-filled afternoon, the cats settled down in a cozy pile, exhausted but happy. They had discovered not just lost toys but also the joy of play and togetherness. Darin and Tessa smiled at their contented fur babies, knowing that sometimes cleaning could lead to the best adventures.

Chapter 14: Belly Time with Papa

As the sun set, the house settled into evening. The family gathered to watch TV and unwind after a busy day.

Deano and Frankie, always eager to snuggle, made their way to the couch. They curled up next to Mama Tessa, their purring creating a gentle symphony of contentment. As they nestled in, Deano gently rubbed his wet nose against Mama's sweet cheek, a gesture to show his love.

"This is the best spot," he purred, nuzzling closer to her side.

Samy, with his calm and relaxed demeanor, had a favorite spot of his own—right on Papa's belly. Every night was "belly time," and Samy loved to sprawl out comfortably, soaking in the warmth and affection. He rubbed his wet nose against Papa's hand, a sign of his fondness.

"You know I wouldn't trade this for the world," Darin said, chuckling as he scratched Samy's chin. Samy would look at Mama, and she would say, *"Thank you for accepting and loving Papa."*

In return, Samy gently blinked—and in cat language, that was his way of saying, *"I love you."*

As the family settled in, the TV flickered, casting a soft glow. They watched their favorite show and laughed together. Deano and Frankie occasionally glanced up at the colorful images but mostly snuggled, rubbing their noses against Mama and Papa to share their love.

Between episodes, Mama whispered to the brothers, *"You two are the best cuddle buddies,"* and Deano responded with a soft purr.

Frankie blinked slowly, a sign of trust and love, as he nestled deeper into Mama's side, giving her a gentle nudge with his wet nose.

Chapter 15: A New Day, A New Joy

Before the first rays of sunshine paint the sky, our little Deano begins his morning mission.

With soft paws and a gentle, determined meow, he tiptoes across us, weaving his way up the bed like a tiny, purring explorer. Frankie, ever the snoozer, remains curled up by my feet, grumbling for just a few more minutes of sleep. Darin, half-awake and laughing, always protests: *"Deano, it's still dark outside — not playtime yet!"*

But Deano is unstoppable.

He nudges, he purrs, he delivers the tiniest love bites on our noses and cheeks. And like clockwork, I surrender with a smile, sitting up to greet him.

"Who wants to kiss Mama?" I ask, already knowing the answer.

Without hesitation, Deano hops like a little bunny, rubbing his face against mine again and again, his joy practically lighting up the room. We giggle. We cuddle. We start the day wrapped in pure, unfiltered love.

How could you not wake up smiling? Deano knows. He knows it's another day to live, to love, and to share his magic with us — the family who saved him, and the family he saves every single morning.

Chapter 16: The Quest for the Lost Collar

One sunny morning, the cats were playing in the garden when Frankie noticed something was missing.

"Where's my favorite collar?" he asked, looking around frantically. The other cats stopped what they were doing, realizing they hadn't seen Frankie's collar in a while.

"We need to find it!" Billie declared, her eyes determined. "Let's retrace your steps, Frankie! Where did you last see it?"

Frankie thought hard. "I remember wearing it when we were playing by the herb garden, but I'm not sure when it came off."

The cats quickly agreed to help him look for it. They decided to start their search in the garden, checking all the spots where Frankie might have played. They searched under bushes, in the flower beds, and even around the big oak tree, but the collar was nowhere to be found. Frustrated but not ready to give up, Frankie suddenly remembered,

"Maybe I dropped it in the catio*!"* The cats exchanged excited looks, ready for the next adventure. *"Let's go back to the* catio*!"*

Tessa was in the kitchen cooking dinner, so they had to sneak past the kitchen quietly. Finally, they made it back to the catio. They started searching—first on top of the cat tree, then under the cabinets, and between the shelves. Frankie and Samy checked every corner.

Just when they were about to give up, Tessa came in and said, *"Frankie, wear your collar, please,"* and she gently hung it around his neck with a smile.

"See, you look so handsome with your collar!" she added, giving him a hug.

Frankie looked at Mama with love and gave her smooches. Deano laughed and said, *"Mama had it the whole time!"* Mama went back to the kitchen, humming happily.

Frankie jumped for joy and said, *"Thank you, everyone!"*

Chapter 17: Gifts of Gratitude

One eventful morning, the cats woke to the sound of chirping birds and the gentle rustle of leaves outside. As they stretched and yawned, Tessa called out,

"Come quickly! You won't believe what's on the porch!"

The cats rushed to the front door, curious about the surprise. When they stepped outside, they found several small gifts left on the porch.

"Look at all these treasures!" Deano exclaimed. There were colorful feathers, tiny shiny rocks, and, of course, a few dead lizards—courtesy of Billie. The stray cats had left these gifts to thank Mama Tessa and the humans for their kindness.

Billie strutted over to Mama Tessa, her tail held high, as if to say, *"Aren't you impressed?"*

Tessa knelt to pet her and said, "Thank you, Billie! I really appreciate your gifts, even if they are a bit… unconventional."

Billie purred, clearly pleased with the recognition.

Later, as the cats lounged on the porch, Frankie turned to Billie. "I think it's so sweet of you to leave us gifts, but maybe next time you could bring something a little less… creepy?" he suggested with a giggle.

Billie tilted her head, as if considering the words. *"But I love the lizards!"* she replied, her eyes gleaming mischievously.

As the day went on, the cats continued to discover more gifts left by their stray friends. This time, they found a few flying bugs, including a butterfly and some small moths. *"Look at these!"* Deano exclaimed, fluttering his paws in excitement. *"They're just like the flies we catch inside the house!"*

The cats decided to have a little fun with their new flying friends.

"Let's see who can catch the most bugs!" Samy proposed.

The cats sprang into action, darting around the porch, trying to catch the butterflies and moths. Billie was especially good at it, her hunting skills impressive as she leaped and pounced.

After their bug-catching adventure, the cats settled down, feeling happy and grateful for the gifts from their stray friends.

"We're lucky to have such thoughtful friends," Deano said, his eyes shining. "They really appreciate all we do for them."

The other cats nodded in agreement, feeling the warmth of friendship. As the sun began to set, casting a golden glow over the porch, Tessa came outside with a small treat for the cats.

"Thank you all for being such wonderful companions," she said with a smile.

The cats purred in response, grateful for the love and care they received. As the day came to an end, the cats snuggled together, feeling grateful for their home, their humans, and the stray cats who brought them joy.

"Let's always remember to show our appreciation for each other," Billie said, her eyes twinkling. "Even if it means bringing home a few lizards now and then!"

WELCOME

Chapter 18: Artistic Adventures with Frankie

One rainy afternoon, the indoor cats were feeling a bit bored as they watched the raindrops race down the window. Just then, Mama Tessa entered the room carrying a large box.

"I have something special for you all today!" she announced, catching the cats' attention. Mama Tessa opened the box to reveal colorful acrylic paints, canvases, and, of course, catnip.

"Today, you're going to help Frankie create some amazing artwork!" she explained. The cats' eyes widened in excitement, imagining the fun they would have. Frankie, the biggest fan of Mama Tessa when it came to painting, was especially thrilled. He often watched her create beautiful artwork and sometimes sat next to her for hours, mesmerized.

"I can't wait to make beautiful paintings!" Frankie said, bouncing on his paws.

Mama Tessa explained her unique technique: "We'll put the paint on the canvas, place it in a zip lock, and then add catnip on top. You'll all help create the art by rubbing and rolling all over it!"

Mama Tessa set up the canvases and poured bright colors of paint onto them. The cats watched in fascination as the colors swirled together. She then placed each canvas inside a large zip lock bag and sprinkled catnip on top.

"Now it's your turn!" she encouraged. As soon as the catnip was added, the indoor cats couldn't resist. One by one, they pounced onto the zip locks, rolling and rubbing their fur against the bags.

"This is so much fun!" Deano exclaimed, his belly wiggling with delight as he rolled into the catnip.

Frankie led the way, showing everyone how to create beautiful patterns with their movements. With each roll and rub, the paints mix, creating vibrant designs.

"Look at these colors!" Deano said, his eyes wide with wonder as he admired the patterns forming on the canvas.

After they finished creating their masterpieces, Mama Tessa carefully took the canvases out of the zip locks. The cats gathered around, eager to see the results of their artistic efforts.

"Wow! They look amazing!" Samy exclaimed, his eyes shining with pride.

To celebrate their artistic achievements, Mama Tessa set up a mini art gallery in the living room. She hung the paintings on the walls for everyone to see.

"These are truly masterpieces, thanks to all of you!" she said, beaming with pride.

As the afternoon sun peeked through the clouds, the cats felt a sense of accomplishment.

"We should do this again!" Frankie suggested, his tail flicking with excitement. "Art is so much fun, especially when we do it together!"

Soho
"Elephant"
by Frankie Sinatro

Chapter 19: The Whiskered Art Fair

One lazy afternoon, while lounging in their cozy living room, the cats overheard Mama Tessa talking on the phone. *"Yes, we'd love to help with the pet adoption event at the shelter this weekend! I can set up a table with my paintings, and I will donate all proceeds to the shelter,"* she said.

The cats perked up, curious about what this could mean.

Tessa explained that the shelter was close to their hearts, just like it was for their friends who often helped by selling art to support the animals.

After Tessa hung up, she told the cats they would be helping at the Cat Shelter's pet adoption day. *"You all need to be on your best behavior,"* she said. The cats were excited at the thought of making new friends.

The cats wanted to make the event special, so they brainstormed ideas. "We can set up our own table and sell our paintings!" Deano suggested. "And we can make a sign that says all proceeds will go to our treat fund!" Frankie added.

Everyone agreed eagerly, excited to show their artwork to the world. *"After all, Mama Tessa said our artwork is purrfect and extraordinary,"* Samy added.

On the day of the event, the cats arrived at the shelter with Mama Tessa and Papa Darin.

The place was bustling with people, and many cats were eager to find their forever homes.

The Cat Pack immediately got to work, setting up a rest area with toys and blankets.

As the event started, the cats interacted with visitors. *"You're all so cute!"* said an elderly person passing by, smiling warmly. The cats took turns sharing stories about the animals. *"This kitten loves to play with yarn!"* Deano said, showing off a playful kitty. *"And this kitten is very cuddly!"* Frankie added, holding a fluffy kitten close.

Their enthusiasm helped attract more people to the adoption area.

While they played, the cats noticed Mama Tessa talking to customers about her paintings and her inspiration. They watched eagerly as she shared the stories behind each piece.

"Look at how happy she is when she makes a sale!" Samy said, his tail flicking with excitement. "More sales mean more treats for us!" Deano chimed in, grinning at the thought.

As the day went on, Mama Tessa surprised the cats with a special treat—cat-friendly cupcakes!

"You all did such a wonderful job helping today," she said, handing out the treats. The cats cheered, grateful for the yummy reward. By the end of the day, Frankie looked around at their newfound friends and the happy families taking them home.

"We really made a difference today," Tessa said, her heart full of joy. As they headed home, the cats discussed how wonderful it felt to help others, just like their human friends who painted to support the shelter.

"We should do this more often!" Samy suggested. "There are so many animals that need our help!"

Paintings

Chapter 20: The 84th Day

Day 84, the day we've been waiting for. The last treatment. The last countdown. The beginning of everything after.

It feels like a lifetime ago now, but I still remember Day One like it was yesterday. Deano didn't know what was coming, only that we were hovering, our voices too soft, my hands too careful. He looked up at us, eyes wide with suspicion. He immediately tried to wiggle his way out of being held. His meows got louder, a cry for help.

Frankie, his forever protector, pacing back and forth and not knowing what was happening.

We tried everything. Gentle words, a new toy, his favorite treats. But how do we explain to a cat what we are about to do? This strange, sharp, scary thing is going to save his life?

MAY 2024
SUN MON TUE WED THU FRI SAT
84th Day
Deano

Deano was full of life that morning. He leapt onto the cat tree with confidence, his amber eyes gleaming. There was still a cautious glint in his gaze, as if he remembered the hard days, the needles, and the medicine. But it was no longer fear; it was awareness. And he carried it like a badge of courage.

He wasn't the only one celebrating.

Frankie was weaving around him with excitement, purring and batting at toys. Samy sat tall, dignified, on the upper perch, watching with warm approval. And Billie, our sweet, giving Billie, watched it all from her favorite perch near the window. Her eyes sparkled with delight, and her tail curled with anticipation.

Outside, the sun streamed in. The room was warm and full of light, full of life. We had made it. I looked at all of them: Deano, the little warrior; Frankie, the loyal protector; Samy, the wise guardian; and Billie, once a shadow, now a cherished member of our family.

They had all played a part. And today, it was more than just an end to treatment. It was the beginning of the rest of their lives—together, happy, and full of adventure yet to come.

Deano, our FIP survivor and warrior, is all ready for a stroll in the neighborhood to announce his happy news!

5
Life is a wonlerful
journey with the
best of friends.
—The Cat Pack

Chapter 21: You Are Not Alone

The days were long. The nights—longer still.

When Deano first showed signs of illness, we didn't know what we were facing. The sparkle in his eyes had dulled, his energy faded, and his purrs became faint whispers in the quiet hours. What followed was a whirlwind of worry, vet visits, unanswered questions, and a diagnosis that once meant goodbye: **FIP**—Feline Infectious Peritonitis.

But we didn't say goodbye. We said, not today.

Deano's Fight

Deano began daily injections of an antiviral medication called **GS-441524**—a life-saving treatment not yet approved by the FDA in all countries but used successfully worldwide. With every injection came a little more strength, a little more light behind those amber eyes.

We counted the days—

Day 1. Day 21. Day 42. Day 84.

And then... joy. He made it.

Deano, our brave, gentle boy, beat the odds. He is here because we didn't give up—because **you don't give up on family**.

Understanding FIP: A Guide for Cat Guardians What is FIP?

Feline Infectious Peritonitis (FIP) is a serious, often misunderstood

disease caused by a mutation of the feline coronavirus (FCoV). While most cats carry the benign version of the virus and show no symptoms, a small percentage, especially those with weakened immune systems—develop the mutated, 7-dangerous form: FIP.

FIP is not contagious in its mutated form, but the original coronavirus can spread in multi-cat environments (like shelters or foster homes). FIP typically affects young cats, but it can appear in cats of any age.

There are two main forms of FIP:

Wet (effusive): Characterized by fluid buildup in the abdomen or chest, leading to breathing difficulty or a swollen belly.

Dry (non-effusive): Affects organs like the brain, eyes, liver, and kidneys, often leading to neurological symptoms or vision changes.

Symptoms to Watch For:

- Persistent fever unresponsive to antibiotics
- Weight loss and decreased appetite
- Lethargy
- Difficulty breathing or swollen belly (wet form)
- Uncoordinated movement, seizures, or eye inflammation (dry form)

Is There a Cure?

Yes, and this is the part many still don't know: **FIP is now treatable.**

Since 2019, breakthrough antiviral treatments have brought hope and healing to thousands of cats worldwide. GS-441524 (also known simply as "GS") is an antiviral drug that targets the replication of the mutated coronavirus responsible for FIP.

Although not yet FDA-approved in the U.S. (as of 2025), it is widely accessible through global FIP networks, and some versions are available via veterinary supervision in certain countries.

Treatment Overview:

- A typical treatment course lasts **84 days**, with daily subcutaneous injections or oral capsules.
- Success rates are currently estimated at over **85–90%**, especially when treatment begins early.
- Regular bloodwork is needed to monitor liver enzymes, red and white blood cell counts, and other markers.

Global Support and Resources

You're not alone. There is a worldwide network of caregivers, vets, and advocates offering guidance and emotional support.

□? **FIP Warriors®**

One of the most trusted and active global FIP support groups. They offer:

- Treatment guidance
- Vet referrals
- Emotional support
- Success stories

☐ **FIP Warriors®**

- **Website:** fipwarriors.com
- **Facebook Group:** FIP Warriors® 5.0
- **Email:** fipwarriors@gmail.comFIP WarriorsFacebook

FIP Warriors® is a global volunteer network providing support, treatment guidance, and community for those affected by FIP. They primarily operate through their Facebook group and email. FIP Warriors were highly recommended by our Vet. We got our resources and help from this group.

Global Help Contact:

sK☐s Cure FIP™ USA

- **Phone/WhatsApp:** +1 (646) 653-2654
- **Email:** usa@curefip.com
- **Website:** curefipusa.comCureFIP.com+6CURE FIP USA+6CURE FIP OCEANIA+6

They offer free guidance on treatment, dosage, and recovery. You can reach them via phone, WhatsApp, or email. CURE FIP USACURE FIP USA

☐?☐ **Cure FIP™ Global Contacts**

- **Europe Email:** europe@curefip.com
- **Oceania Email:** oceania@curefip.com
- **Oceania WhatsApp:** +61 420 722 953CureFIP.com+6CURE FIP OCEANIA+6CureFIP.com+6

For international support, Cure FIP™ has dedicated contacts for different regions. CureFIP.com

Raising Awareness

Share your cat's story

Talk to your vet about FIP treatment updates

Help others recognize the symptoms early

Advocate for legal access to GS-based medications in all countries

In Memory and Hope

For every cat lost to FIP, there's a survivor who inspires us to keep going.

Every informed guardian becomes a lifeline.

Deano's journey stands as a testament to resilience and the advancements in FIP treatment. By sharing his story, we honor the memory of those lost and inspire hope for those still fighting.

"We didn't give up—and Deano didn't either." – Tessa Cervantes, proud FIP survivor mom.

FIP Awareness Day – November 18

FIP Awareness Day is recognized each year on **November 18** in memory of the groundbreaking work of **Dr. Niels Pedersen**, the pioneering veterinarian, and researcher who devoted over 50 years to studying feline coronaviruses and led the way to finding a treatment for FIP.

This day is about:

- Honoring FIP fighters and survivors like Deano
- Remembering the ones lost too soon
- Spreading awareness about symptoms, diagnosis, and current treatment options
- Rallying for global access to legal, affordable medications

- Connecting cat parents with life-saving communities and support groups

November 18 is FIP Awareness Day – share, speak out, and help save *lives*.

The Author and the Cat Pack

I'm Tessa Cervantes, an artist known as *The Abstract Thinker*. For over 28 years, I've poured my heart into painting, expressing emotion and energy through brushstrokes. But something unexpected happened, and a new creative door opened: writing—another way to express my abstract thinking.

Painting has always helped me see beyond the obvious. Every stroke held a story, a glimpse into something deeper. Writing became an extension of that vision—a new way to tell stories that are real but laced with a little magic. Another dimension of who I am.

My love for cats has shaped this journey more than I could have imagined. Their presence fills my world with quiet wisdom, comfort, and so much inspiration. They've taught me to slow down, notice the little things, and believe in the wonder of the everyday.

And now, I often catch myself wondering: *What comes next, beyond this awakening?*

The possibilities are endless if you believe in yourself. – Tessa

Got a comment or a heartwarming message? Email me at:

whiskerwinkspress@gmail.com